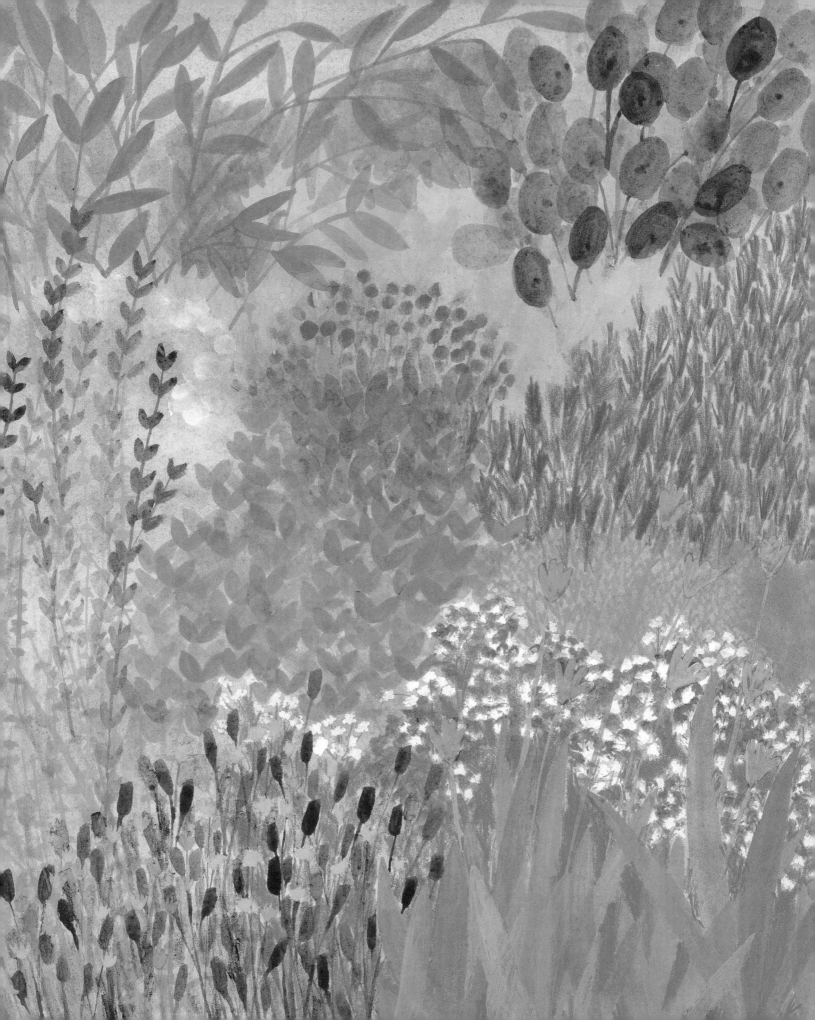

For Sorrel xxx

First published 2021 by Macmillan Children's Books
an imprint of Pan Macmillan
The Smithson, 6 Briset Street, London EC1M 5NR
EU representative: Macmillan Publishers Ireland Limited,
Mallard Lodge, Lansdowne Village, Dublin 4
Associated companies throughout the world.
www.panmacmillan.com

ISBN: 978-1-4472-5053-1 (HB)
ISBN: 978-1-4472-5054-8 (PB)

Text and illustrations copyright © Rebecca Cobb 2021

1 3 5 7 9 8 6 4 2

A CIP catalogue record for this book is available from the British Library.

Printed in China.

With thanks to Hannah, Lydia, Louise,
Sam, Kit, Sorrel, Mum and Richard.

FSC
www.fsc.org

MIX
Paper from
responsible sources
FSC® C116313

Aunt Amelia's House

Rebecca Cobb

MACMILLAN CHILDREN'S BOOKS

We were very excited! We were going to stay with Aunt Amelia.

We had never been to her house before,
and we were going all by ourselves!

Although we would miss Mum and Dad,
we knew we would have a brilliant time.

The journey was rather long,

but finally we arrived.

We said goodbye to Mum and Dad, and then
asked Aunt Amelia what fun things she had planned.

"Well," she said, "I'm afraid there are lots of jobs to do."

It didn't sound much fun,
and it wasn't at all what we had imagined.

But it looked like Aunt Amelia
could do with our help.
"Let's start with the garden," she said.

The garden was ENORMOUS . . .

but Aunt Amelia had a good way of
watering all the plants quickly.

Afterwards, we picked lots of fruit.
"Let's share it with the neighbours,"
Aunt Amelia said.

They were very pleased.

Next, it was time to feed Aunt Amelia's pets.
It took quite a while.

Then we worked very hard
doing some more chores.

Inside . . .

. . . and out.

Finally, there was dinner to make before sitting down to eat it.

Once everyone had gone home, Aunt Amelia
smiled. "Thank you for your help with all
those jobs," she said. "Now, how about
playing some games before bedtime?"

The next day, Mum and Dad came to collect us.

"We hope you had a lovely time?" asked Mum.

"Have they been good?" asked Dad.

"Invaluable," said Aunt Amelia.

On the way home, Dad said, "We thought you might like to go out somewhere fun today?"

"Thank you," we said. "That's really kind . . .

"... but we are afraid that we have lots of jobs to do!"

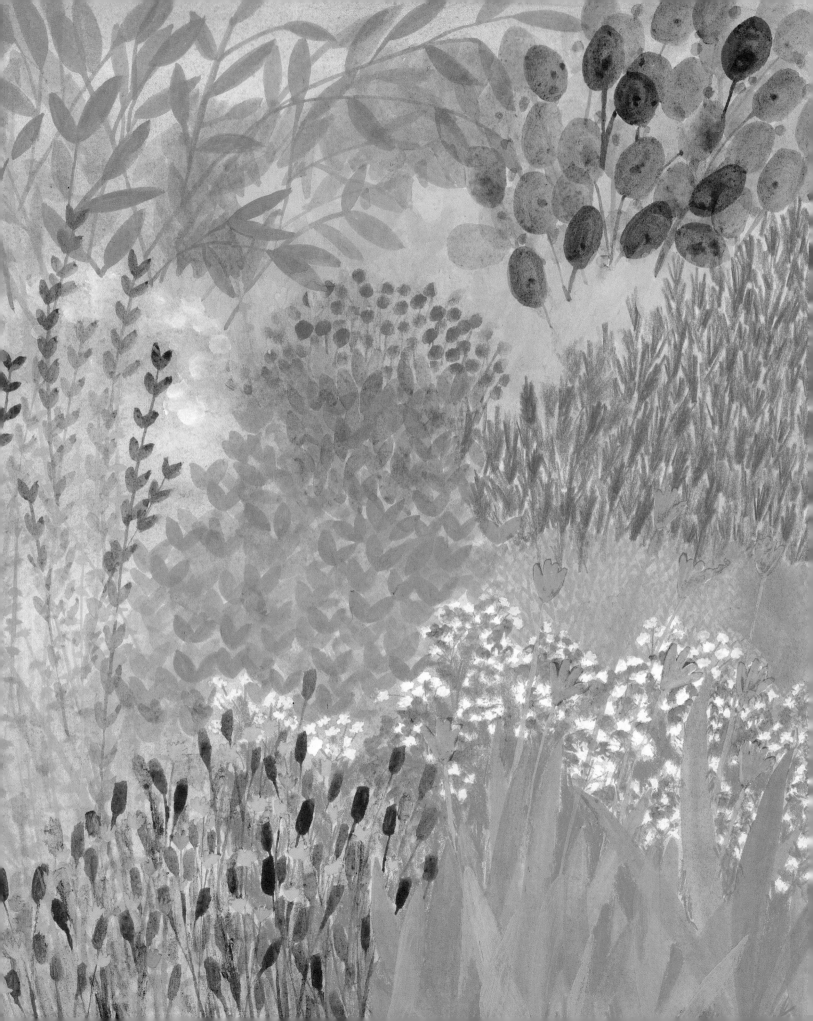